Caleb S. Henry

The Endless Future of the Human Race

A letter to a friend

Caleb S. Henry

The Endless Future of the Human Race
A letter to a friend

ISBN/EAN: 9783337368425

Printed in Europe, USA, Canada, Australia, Japan

Cover: Foto ©Andreas Hilbeck / pixelio.de

More available books at **www.hansebooks.com**

THE

ENDLESS FUTURE

OF THE

HUMAN RACE.

A LETTER TO A FRIEND.

BY

C. S. HENRY, D. D.

NEW YORK:

D. APPLETON AND COMPANY,

549 AND 551 BROADWAY.

1879.

PREFACE.

THE following letter to a friend was written several months before Canon Farrar's "Sermons on Eternal Hope" were preached, and before the article in the "North American Review" on "The Doctrine of Eternal Punishment" was published. It was specially intended, not for scholars or theological doctors, but for a large and increasing class of readers "of average thoughtfulness and intelligence" who were brought up in the traditional orthodox doctrine, but now find themselves troubled and distressed in the attempt to hold it.

In what I have said with respect to the exegetical question, "What does the New Testament teach concerning the *duration* of future punishment?" I have quoted a good many passages from a little book entitled "Is Eternal Punishment endless?" which I referred to as put out anonymously, but which since then has come to a second edition, and is understood to have been written by Dr. Whiton. I have not seen this second edition. On the *exegetical* question I entirely agree with the views Dr. Whiton presents. On this question I have for twenty years held the same view with him; and in my letter I have gladly availed myself of the opportunity of quoting many of his expressions so forcibly put and so admirable for their spirit.

I suppose my little tract contains a good many things from which a great many persons may dissent. I am sensible that I have not proposed nor attempted to dispose of *all* the difficulties of the subject. It was not within the scope of my purpose to do so. I hope, however, that what I have said will be clearly intelligible to all my readers, and that my treatment of the subject will not be objected to as wanting in fairness, modesty, and reverence. I wish my tract may be regarded not as a polemic discussion so much as a brief suggestive expression of the reasons one may find for reverently entertaining a humble hope and trust in the final triumph of Infinite Divine Love over all sin and suffering in the universe.

STAMFORD, CONNECTICUT, *November*, 1878.

CONTENTS.

		PAGE
1.	INTRODUCTORY	7
2.	"FUTURE PUNISHMENT"	8
3.	THE DURATION OF FUTURE PUNISHMENT	9
4.	THE EXEGETICAL INQUIRY	12
5.	AN OPEN QUESTION	22
6.	THE REASONS FOR MY HOPE	24
7.	PROBATION IN THE WORLD TO COME	30
8.	PROBATIONARY DISCIPLINE	32
9.	PURGATORY, BUT NOT THE ROMISH ONE	34
10.	PRAYING FOR THE DEAD	36
11.	HELL—HADES—GEHENNA	38
12.	THROUGH PAIN TO PENITENCE	41
13.	THE WORM AND THE FIRE	41
14.	FINALE	44

APPENDICES.

I.	MODERN ORTHODOX REPRESENTATIONS OF FUTURE PUNISHMENT	47
II.	MEDIÆVAL OPINION	58
III.	RECENT ROMAN CATHOLIC REPRESENTATIONS	64
IV.	ALEXANDER EWING, BISHOP OF ARGYLL AND THE ISLES	73

ENDLESS FUTURE OF THE HUMAN RACE.

1. Introductory.

MY DEAR FRIEND: You tell me you believe—
as you know I do—in the being of God as the
eternal author, upholder, and ruler of the universe, infinite in power, wisdom, and goodness.
You tell me also you agree with me in believing
that God has destined all his spiritual creatures
to an endless duration of existence; and you ask
me whether I believe the common "orthodox"
doctrine, that the fate of myriads of the human
race—the great bulk, indeed, of mankind—will be
one of never-ending sin and suffering in the world
beyond the grave. To this question I frankly
answer, No; on the contrary, I say without hesitation that I humbly hope and trust that the
endless existence of every human being will, in
point of actual fact, become ultimately one of
endless goodness and blessedness.

That the orthodox doctrine should have gained

and maintained for ages such a hold as it has had on the faith of the Christian world must be mainly attributed to the fact that *it has been believed to be a divinely revealed doctrine taught by Christ and his apostles;* for nothing short of this can sufficiently account for the acceptance of a doctrine so awful in itself, so overwhelming to the imagination, so frightfully repugnant to every one's instinctive desire of happiness for himself, and so shocking to the sensibilities of every one who loves his fellow creatures. Whether Christ and his apostles have really taught this doctrine is a point I propose to consider. But first I have something to say with respect to the sufferings ordained for sinful men in the world beyond the grave, considered apart from the question of their duration.

2. *"Future Punishment."*

These words, in a just construction of their meaning, express a doctrine of natural religion which is proclaimed in the spiritual constitution of the human soul : in the absolute ideas of right and wrong ; of obligation and responsibility, merit and demerit, guilt and ill desert ; and in that experience of remorse which (often so terribly) accompanies the consciousness of ill desert—in these we recognize the voice of God speaking in the universal mind and heart of mankind. It is nothing strange, therefore, that the belief in a state

of future retribution has prevailed in every age of
the world and in all nations, the rude and barbar-
ous as well as the civilized and cultivated; and in
proportion as the higher degrees of culture have
been reached, heathen philosophers have framed
rational demonstrations, heathen moralists have
uttered solemn admonitions, and heathen poets
have sung in fearful strains of the destination of
men to a judgment beyond the grave.

And what natural religion teaches Christianity
unquestionably proclaims. Jesus Christ himself
has so far drawn aside the veil that hangs between
the present and the future as to disclose to us
some glimpses of a place or state of suffering in
the world beyond the grave. The images he em-
ploys are quite fearful. But it avails nothing to
say they are only images, mere metaphorical expressions. What as matter of fact they mean to
declare, is the question. About this there can be
no doubt. They declare a reality and severity of
suffering appointed for sinful men proportioned to
every one's character, deserts, and needs.

3. *The Duration of Future Punishment.*

As to the duration of future punishment I do
not think natural religion speaks decisively. It
appears to me there is nothing in the necessary
dictates of reason—nothing in the idea of God and
a moral government, nothing in the sacred principles of eternal justice, nothing in the nature of sin

or in the degree of any sinner's guilt—which goes to demand or to justify an unqualified assertion on the subject. So far as reason and reasonable considerations go, it seems to me that all that can be rightly said is that future punishment may possibly be endless, and it may possibly not be so. These opposite possibilities both stand in the fact that, as in this life, so in the life to come, individual character must determine individual destiny. The principles of a just divine administration demand that it shall go well with the righteous, but the wicked shall be in evil plight; and by the constitution of the human soul sin and misery are inseparably wedded together: to be bad is in itself to be badly off. It is so in this life. It must needs be so in the life to come. Whoever passes from this world evil in character must, in the world beyond the grave, find himself in a condition of corresponding ill-being or suffering which will last as long as he continues evil in character. This may possibly be forever. But on the other hand his character may become changed from wickedness to goodness, and thereby from wretchedness to happiness.

So much for what reason reasonably determines. And as to Christianity, it is undeniable that it teaches, as I have said, a severe doctrine on the sufferings of the wicked in the world to come. But does it positively teach that there is to be no end to these sufferings? Does it declare anything

more positive and absolute than what reason suggests and declares, namely, the hypothetical possibility of an endless self-willed individual persis-
tence in evil, and the consequent endless misery it
must entail ? Or, in other words, does Christianity
teach that in point of fact every human being who
passes into the other world evil in character will
continue forever evil and forever suffer the mis-
eries of hell ?

This is a question purely of the interpretation
of the meaning of the original language of the
New Testament. Our English version expresses
only the opinions of the translators as to the meaning of the original. They may be right or they
may be wrong in their rendering—as all translators are liable to be. It may indeed be admitted—
and should be—that one may get from our English
translation a sufficiently correct impression with
respect to the *fact* and the *severity* of the sufferings ordained for sinful men in the world beyond
the grave. But not so with respect to the *duration* of those sufferings. This is a point not to be
determined merely from the language of any translation *assumed* to be a correct version of the original language of the New Testament. For the
previous question is precisely whether the version
is correct. This is a question that can be determined only by confronting the original language
of the New Testament. It settles nothing to flash
before men's eyes the words of our English trans-

lation and exclaim, "Everlasting is everlasting," "Eternal is eternal." Nor is anything settled by a remarkable argument I have lately seen * which asserts that the New Testament teaches the endlessness of future punishment because Christians have universally or nearly universally believed, and do believe, that it does so teach. For the principle on which the argument proceeds (even if the alleged universality of belief were a fact) would, by a parity of reasoning, go to prove that Copernicus and Galileo were heretics for asserting an astronomical theory contrary to the universal Christian belief of their day. The only way to settle the question (if it can be settled) is to ascertain simply as a matter of fact whether the original words employed by Christ and his apostles do actually assert, either expressly or by direct implication, that the duration of the future sufferings of the wicked is to be strictly endless. It is a question of exegesis—of the correct interpretation of the original words. This I feel bound to admit and maintain, and all the more so because it is not my purpose to go into an extended philological discussion.

4. *The Exegetical Inquiry.*

You say you are not a Greek scholar. I do not think it necessary you should be in order to a sufficient appreciation of what I have to say. I

---

* "Sin and Penalty," by Hugh Miller Thompson, pp. 10–12.

take for granted that you do not *wish* to believe in the *endless* duration of future punishment. I take for granted that you and every right-hearted man would be *glad* to be able to believe the contrary. And all I wish to show is that a just construction of the original language of the New Testament does not *oblige* you to believe that it positively teaches the absolute endlessness of the sufferings of sinners in the world to come. It is to this single point that I shall confine myself; nor shall I go into an exhaustive discussion even of this point, but shall only present such a view of it as may suffice to establish what I have just said.

I begin by considering the great text, Matt. xxv. 46. The determination of the meaning of that passage may be taken as determining the question as to all the teaching of the New Testament on the duration of future punishment.

Our English translators have rendered the passage: " These shall go away into everlasting punishment: but the righteous into life eternal." In doing so they have undoubtedly expressed their opinion that our Lord intended to declare positively the endless duration of future punishment. Taken in this sense, is their translation a correct one? The answer turns on the meaning of a single word; for, though our translators have used two words—" everlasting " in the first clause, and " eternal " in the second — yet in the original there is but one and the same word. That word is *aἰώνιος, æonian*. Putting this word in both clauses, the passage would read : " These shall go away into *æonian* punishment: but the righteous into *æonian* life." What reason our translators had for using *two* different epithets to translate this one single word of the original is not perfectly clear. But it is certain that if they had translated the word in both clauses by the epithet *endless* they would have expressed precisely what they took to be the meaning of the original—so far as respects *duration*.

Does, then, the original word in this passage necessarily mean endless? This raises the question whether, in the usage of the original writers of the New Testament, and of the Greek (Septuagint) translation of the Old Testament, the adjective *æonian* is an unambiguous word, of invariable signification, and when relating to duration always strictly and properly signifying a duration that is absolutely endless. Now, every scholar knows that such is not the fact. It is an ambiguous word of very variable signification. It is used in a great variety of meanings, both in the Greek (Septuagint) translation of the Old Testament and in the original Greek of the New Testament.

I can not express the result to which I have been led, by a careful and, I think, unprejudiced examination of the original language of the New Testament, better than by citing the words of a very scholar-like and able little treatise entitled " Is Eternal Punishment endless ? " — put out anonymously.* The writer says that "the adjective *æonian*, neither by itself nor by what it derives from its noun *æon*, gives any testimony to the endlessness of future punishment. Futurity being represented in the New Testament as a succession of æons, ' æonian punishment '—so far as the phrase itself can carry its own interpretation—is altogether of indefinite duration ; all that the definition ' æonian ' gives with any certainty being this, that the punishment *belongs to* or *occurs in* the æon or the æons to come " (pp. 16, 17).

Among the great number of those whose opinions on this point may be thought to have a certain force of authority, I will refer you only to two, than whom, on a question of sacred exegesis, none can have greater weight. Dr. Pusey, as eminent for his Biblical learning as venerable for his character, says that the word *æonian* can not rightly be translated as absolutely " everlasting." And the late Dr. Tayler Lewis, equally eminent for " orthodoxy " and for scholarship, says : " Æonian, from its adjective form, may perhaps mean an existence, a duration, measured by *æons* or worlds, just as our present world or æon is measured by years or centuries. But it would be more in accordance with the plainest etymological usage

* Published by Lockwood, Brooks & Co , Boston, 1876.

to give it simply the sense of *æonic*, denoting the
world to come. 'These shall go away into the
punishment [the restraint, imprisonment] of the
world to come, and these into the life of the world
to come.' This is all we can etymologically or
exegetically make of the word in this passage"
(Matt. xxv.).* In this connection Dr. Lewis ad-
verts to the "aspect of finality" which is pre-
sented to us in the scene portrayed in that passage. No doubt it has such an aspect. No doubt
the same is true in many other passages. But
this raises the question "whether this finality is
relative or *absolute*. Does it cover merely an *indefinite* period, however protracted, or a duration
that never comes to a period?"† On this point
(the question, namely, of absolute finality) there
is something I may well refer those to who take
the Mosaic account (Gen. ii. 17) for a literal history. God is there represented as declaring, "In
the day thou eatest thereof thou shalt surely die."
Nothing can have more the "aspect of finality"
than this. Yet, immediately after the disobe-
dience of man, there was a *new* dispensation disclosed—the seed of the woman bruising the serpent's head. Why, then, may there not be a
future disclosure which shall show that the *æonian*
punishment of the wicked is not an absolute finality? I trust there will be, though I do not take

* Lewis, excursus in Lange's "Commentary," p. 48.
† "Is Eternal Punishment endless?" p. 35.

the Mosaic record to be literally historical. I have other reasons for my trust.

Before concluding these remarks on Matt. xxv. 46, there is another point to be considered. It is alleged by some that this passage proves the endlessness of the *æonian* punishment by the strongest implication, even though it be admitted that as a direct statement it is not decisive. The argument is, that whatever holds true of the duration of *æonian* "*life*" must hold true of the *æonian* "*punishment*," for "both states," as Professor Lewis says, "are precisely parallel, and we can not exegetically make any difference in the force and extent of the terms." Now this, I grant, would be decisive if "æonian life" denoted merely or primarily a certain *length* of life. But this is not the case. Perpetuity of duration is indeed involved, but in the primary sense of the words "æonian life" signifies a certain *kind* of life—a spiritual state, disposition, or character of the soul. It is so used in a great many passages: as in John v. 24, "He that heareth my word and believeth on him that sent me . . . . *hath* æonian life . . . . *is passed* from death unto life"; John iii. 36, "He that believeth on the Son *hath* æonian life"; 1 John v. 11, 12, "This is the record that God *hath given* us æonian life, and this life is *in* his Son. He that hath the Son [the spirit of the Son] *hath* life; and he that hath not the Son of God *hath not* life"; John

xvii. 3, " This *is* the æonian life, that they may
know thee the only God, and Jesus Christ whom
thou hast sent." All these and such like passages
denote primarily a spiritual state, a *kind* of life
and *not length* of life.

I come now to one consideration more which
goes *decisively to settle the question before us.*

It is a fact which I suppose no competent
scholar will deny, that " the Greek, like the English, has its appropriate words to express with pre-
cision the idea of endlessness. When the endlessness of future punishment was first declared to be
an article of the orthodox faith (A. D. 544), the
word *ateleutetos*, endless, was employed for that
purpose." * And I take it to be undeniable that it
was as easy in the Greek language as it is in the
English to find words to express decisively the
idea of absolute endlessness. We are brought,
therefore, to confront the great question, *Why is
it that in the original language of the New Testament our Lord is represented as using the ambiguous, indeterminate word æonian ?* This is a
question that can not be evaded—it must be met
face to face. And I am bold to say that it is
utterly impossible to give any other reasonable
answer to the question than this : that it was because *our Lord intended* NOT *to make a decisive
declaration as to the duration of future punish-*

---

* " Is Eternal Punishment endless ? " p. 8.

ment. Whatever his reasons were for leaving the question undecided, it is certain that his words, " These shall go away into *æonian* punishment," do not oblige me to *believe* in the absolute endlessness of that punishment, any more than they authorize me to *disbelieve* in it. One thing, however, is certain, namely, that they give me a perfect right to deny that he has in this great passage decisively TAUGHT the endless duration of future punishment, and leave me at liberty to entertain whatever opinion on that point I find good ground in reason for adopting. So much with respect to the meaning of Matt. xxv. 46.

There are other passages in the New Testament relating to future punishment in which the epithet *æonian* is found. But " none of the words which we find coupled with the epithet—such as ' æonian *fire*' (Matt. xviii. 8), or ' æonian *damnation*,' or ' æonian *judgment*' (Heb. vi. 2)—adds any further definiteness to the indefinite adjective." *

But are there not other statements which explicitly or by implication go decisively to determine the question which our Lord, in Matt. xxv. 46, left undetermined ? On this point the writer just referred to says : " As to explicit statements, there are some which *our version* makes quite as decisive as it takes the passage Matt. xxv. 46 to be ; but in the *original* they are equally indeterminate. In Mark ix. 43, for instance, we read

* " Is Eternal Punishment endless ? " p. 18.

of 'the fire that never shall be quenched.' The
word 'never' is a contribution of our translators
to the original *asbestos*. This may be translated
'unquenched' as correctly as 'unquenchable.'
And even if we call it 'unquenchable,' this epithet is equally open to a limited interpretation.
We often say that a conflagration 'raged with
unquenchable fury,' meaning that it could not be
quenched till its material was consumed. The
epithet *asbestos* is applicable to a fire that lasts
very long, or a fire that is for a time beyond all
control, as fairly as to a fire that is literally endless. How, then, do we know that the latter is the
real meaning of our Lord's word ? . . .

"A similar addition to the limited force of the
original has been made by the translators in Mark
iii. 29, 'hath *never* forgiveness,' etc. The original, in the most approved text, reads 'hath not
forgiveness for the æon, but is involved in an
æonian sin.' The idea is stated more explicitly in
the parallel text in Matt. xii. 32, where the original, fairly rendered in our version, reads 'it
shall not be forgiven him either in this æon or in
the one to be.' It is remarkable that St. Augustine himself derived from this text the idea that
in the coming æon some would obtain forgiveness
who were unforgiven in the present. . . . We
have, however, observed that the Scriptures speak
of futurity as running its course through 'æons
of æons.' What, then, of him who finds no for-

giveness 'in the æon that is to be' after the present? Are we to *assume* that he will never find it in any succeeding æon? . . . So far from the absolute endlessness of future punishment being taught by these two texts, it is the very point which they abstain from pronouncing.

"Perhaps no text has been more strained beyond its legitimate import, for proof of the endlessness of future punishment, than John iii. 36, 'He that believeth not the Son shall not see life; but the wrath of God abideth on him.' 'Shall *not* see life' is assumed to mean 'shall *never* see life.' 'The wrath of God abideth on him' is assumed to be the same as 'abideth *evermore.*' The text is declared to teach the unbeliever's irrecoverable abandonment to the powers of punishment. . . . But compare 1 John iii. 14, 'He that loveth not his brother abideth in death.' How long? So long as he 'loveth not his brother.' No one presses the extreme inference that every unloving soul in this world abideth irrecoverably in death. What warrant have we for treating the other 'abideth' any differently? . . . It is an abuse of the text to make it declare anything more than the truth that shines on the face of it, namely, that 'he who believeth not the Son shall not see life' *while he remains in unbelief,* 'but the wrath of God abideth on him' *so long as he continues an unbeliever.* Any other interpretation would condemn to final ruin every person in the

world who is at present not a believer in Christ.
And this is the sort of evidence on which many
good people are content, through the force of un-
reflecting habit, to rest the tremendous burden
of the doctrine of an absolutely endless punishment. . . .

"The result of our inquiry thus far is that the
texts which in our *English* Bibles appear to teach
in the plainest manner the endlessness of future
punishment do not seem to teach it in an exact
and unprejudiced interpretation of the original.
The utmost that can be said is, that they leave the
duration of future punishment indefinite; they
abstain from saying that it is absolutely and literally endless." *

So much with respect to the exegetical question.
As expressing my own opinion on this question,
I have, as you may perceive, quoted very largely'
the language of the little treatise to which I have
so often referred.

5. *An Open Question.*

I take it to be undeniable that our Lord has
left the question as to the endlessness of future
punishment an open question. And such it was
regarded in the Christian Church for five hundred
years, during which period "it was not inconsis-
tent with a reputation for orthodoxy to believe and
teach that the 'æonian punishment' would some

* "Is Eternal Punishment endless?" pp. 19 *et seq.*

time terminate. . . . . The endlessness of that punishment was first authoritatively announced as an article of the orthodox creed in the sixth century at the instance of the Emperor Justinian I., an authority in theological matters of equal respectability with that of King Henry VIII." *

The history of the Church of England gives us a significant fact on this subject. In the first draft of the Articles of Religion of that church there was one (the forty-second) which contained a decree affirming the endlessness of future punishment. This article was in the subsequent revision stricken out. The significance of the omission is this: it was, as Mr. Maurice says,† a "careful, considerate omission, in a document for future times, of that which had been too hastily admitted. . . . The omission was made by persons who probably were strong in the belief that the punishment of wicked men is endless, but who did not dare to enforce that opinion upon others." The members of the English Church were thus left at liberty to hold whatever opinion on the subject they saw fit to entertain. From that day to this it has been, and is now, an open question in that church—as also in the Anglo-American daughter church.

Supposing Mr. Maurice to be correct in what he says respecting the personal opinions of the

* "Is Eternal Punishment endless?" p. 78.
† See Maurice, "Theological Essays," pp. 347–349.

revisers who threw out the forty-second article, I
have to remark that there is a sense in which I
am of the same opinion with them—that is to
say, I believe "the punishment of wicked men"
is endless in case the wickedness is endless; but
that wicked men dying in their wickedness are
divinely debarred from any chance of future repentance and restoration to goodness and blessedness (which is what these revisers "probably were
strong in the belief of "), that is something I do
not believe.   On the contrary, as I have said at
the outset, I have a humble hope and trust that
the endless existence of every human being will
ultimately become one of endless goodness and
blessedness.   My reasons for this hope I now pro-
ceed to give you.

6. The Reasons for my Hope.

My hope and trust in the final restoration of
all men to goodness and blessedness are grounded
in my conviction of the infinite goodness of God,
and in the consideration of the immense resources
of influence—compatible with the spiritual freedom of his rational creatures—which his infinite
power and wisdom enable him to employ for ac-
complishing this end.

The goodness of God can not otherwise be
rightly conceived than as consisting in his infinite
love and infinite righteousness, which are the essential elements of his eternal nature.   God is

love. Love is devotion. There is no selfishness
in pure and perfect love; and God's love to mankind is an infinite, unselfish devotion to their
highest well-being. God is righteousness: he is
incapable of doing anything wrong, anything contrary to the principles of absolute and immutable
justice—incapable, therefore, of wronging a single
human being. We are the offspring of God; we
owe our existence to his fatherly love. When
he brought us into being he formed us in his own
spiritual image—making us like himself rational
and free, and so capable of endless goodness and
blessedness. The final cause, therefore, of our existence—the supreme end for which he created
us—was that we might become forever good and
forever blessed. It lies in the very necessity of
his essential goodness that he should desire us'
to realize this supreme end of our being. It must
needs be the dearest wish of his fatherly heart
that every individual of the human race should in
the measure of his capacity become loving and
righteous as he himself is, and so forever blessed
with a spiritual blessedness like his own; and,
moreover, that he must hold himself bound in
righteousness—as well as be prompted by love—
to do everything in his power to secure this end.
He would not otherwise be a God of love and
righteousness. This I am compelled to believe
by the necessity of the reason and conscience he
has made me with.

The thought that the fate of any of the children of the infinitely loving Father should,
through their own self-willed and obstinate resis-
tance to his holy and loving wish and will, be
necessarily one of endless sinfulness and woe—
the thought of this, regarded as a bare theoretical
possibility, is enough to fill the mind and heart
with unutterable awe and sadness. Yet that it
may be so is what must be admitted as a theoretical possibility; for it is a necessary corollary from
the idea of that freedom of the will without
which there could be neither any proper responsibility nor any true goodness of character.

But the thought that it will be actually so in
any case through default of anything which God
could do to prevent it, is monstrous; and still
more monstrous is the thought that it will be so
through any efficient purpose or agency on God's
part to make it so. It is impossible to imagine
anything more utterly abominable—more at vari-
ance with the idea of a good God and more revolting to every just human sentiment—than these
monstrous notions. They make God the infinite
evil one. No matter by what authority my acceptance of them is claimed, I have not a moment's hesitation in rejecting them   It is enough
for me that such notions contradict the eternal
principles of absolute righteousness. No tradition, no amount of historical evidence, no authority of any sort, can rightfully establish the divine

origin of a religion which propounds to our belief things so absolutely contradictory to reason and conscience. I would sooner be an atheist than accept them. Better a chance-medley universe than one controlled by a Supreme Being capable of creating millions of human creatures with a predetermination to condemn them to everlasting misery.

I believe the love of the Infinite Father of spirits embraces every individual of the human race. It is his being and nature to love them all with a love that is as holy as it is tender. Our sinfulness is revolting to him, but it does not destroy his love. He loves us in spite of it, and would fain draw us to repentance and to holiness. Sin-hating, but sinner-loving! Such has ever been, is now, and must forever be, God's heart toward every individual of our race. To his tender love for mankind we owe the method of *salvation* disclosed in the gospel. The only salvation that could save a sin-disordered race must needs be a salvation *from* sin, from its inward, deadly power. Such a salvation God only could provide, and was behooved by his holiness and love to provide. He has done so. He sent his Son into the world to take our nature and in it to live, to suffer, and to die. *Why* this particular method of Divine intervention in our behalf was chosen I can not say, or rather I will not permit myself to speculate about it. Nor am I able to explain *how* it is that Christ's coming, liv-

ing, suffering, and dying effected the salvation of
the human race. The *quo modo* of the efficacious
connection between the coming of Christ and the
potential restoration of the race I can not understand. I adopt the view of Bishop Butler and of
Coleridge—that it is a transcendent fact. I can
indeed understand what is clearly declared, namely, that the mission of Christ was the Infinite Father's method of love to man. This his Son, the
Divine Missionary, came proclaiming: "God so
loved the world that he sent his Son that the
world might through him be saved." Here we
have the great historic truth that God sent his
Son. Here we have the loving motive and the
inestimable benefits procured for man. But I
find no explanation of the *how*. Many theories
have been framed, diverse and conflicting, and
some of them immoral and monstrous. I reject
them all. I do not believe in any wrathful and
avenging God "sheathing his flaming sword in
his Son's vital blood"—according to the words
of good Dr. Watts's pious-impious hymn. I do
not believe in any horrible forensic device for
"satisfying Divine justice" by outraging the inmost principle of righteousness.

God's love and Christ's love! This is all the
theory I find. A salvation provided as wide as
the needs of mankind. What a monstrous doctrine that is which says God sent his Son into
the world that a part only of the world might

through him be saved, leaving the rest, in countless millions, to a foreordained fate of helpless, hopeless, endless perdition! What a doctrine which says that Christ laid down his life not for every man but only for a certain arbitrarily selected number, and that the Holy Ghost, the Sanctifier, is given only to those elected ones! The God that I believe in and trust is one who declares himself "loving unto every man"—whose "tender mercies are over all his works." In the gospel, as I read it, I find disclosed a provision for the salvation of all men, even though the knowledge of the method of it be not *now* imparted to all. Everywhere over all the earth, from the day when the history of humanity began, God has been "in Christ reconciling the world unto himself." Everywhere, in every age, the Spirit of God has wrought in every unresisting human soul to quicken "that *faith* which is the germ of all that is good in human character"—that *implicit* faith, that disposition, which may exist in the heart and will of men to whom the Saviour's name is yet unknown. And so it is said that "in every nation he that feareth God and worketh righteousness"—according to the light that *is in him*—is accepted of him. And whatever knowledge it is necessary for him to have in order to an *explicit* faith in Christ, shall some time—in God's good time—be given; and what is not given in this

world will, I can not doubt, be given in the world
to come.

The Infinite Father has not fully explained his
reasons for leaving the light of the gospel to make
its way through the operation of historical causes,
and with such slow progress and imperfect spread.
But their wisdom and goodness we can not doubt.
One thing we may take for certain : that human
history has from its beginning been conducted
under the superintendence of God's never-failing
providence, and the dispensation of his gracious
Spirit working in every human soul.

Nor can we doubt that throughout the lifetime
of humanity upon the earth the course of human
history will go on upon the same principles as
have presided over it from the beginning.

And as to human history in the world beyond
the grave, I can not doubt that the same principles
will continue to prevail. I can not doubt that so
long as evil shall exist the supreme purpose of
God's government over the human race will be to
overcome evil by good ; that so long as there shall
be souls unsaved from sin, God must needs strive
to save them by all the reclaiming powers of his
providence and grace which his almighty goodness enables him to employ.

7. *Probation in the World to come.*

The idea of a continued probation for the human race in the world beyond the grave underlies

pretty nearly everything I have written.   In what Christ and his apostles have said I find nothing which obliges me to believe that the present life is the only period of probation allotted to mankind; and it seems to me there is nothing in the reason of the case that demands or justifies such a belief.   On the contrary, every analogy of reason —everything in the character of God and in the principles and facts of the Divine administration —goes to justify the presumption of a future state of probation.   What reason—compatible with God's character as a being of infinite holiness and righteousness, love and mercy—can be imagined why he should not carry the dispensation of the gospel into the future world?   Why should he not continue to do there what he is now doing here?   Think how he is dealing with us now, here in this life!   By his gracious Spirit working in every human soul, by the manifold methods of his ever-watchful and all-ordering providence, by the whole discipline of life, he is now always trying to reclaim us from sin to goodness and to himself.   Why, I say, should he not *continue* to deal with us in the world to come as he is dealing with us now?   Why should he stop trying to rescue sinful souls from the dominion and misery of sin merely because they have passed from this world into the world beyond?   Certainly the *event* which we call " death " can not be conceived as making any change in God's loving and merciful disposition toward them. Nor can that event be conceived as working any such change in their spiritual nature or in their character as to make them no longer proper subjects for his Divine mercy, or to put them beyond the reach of his reclaiming efforts.

I can not, therefore, believe the common notion, that the fate of every individual of the human race is unalterably determined for weal or for woe by each one's character at the moment of death. And I can not help entertaining the belief that human probation will be continued in the world beyond the grave.

8. *Probationary Discipline.*

After what I have elsewhere said, I need not add anything here to show that I accept our Lord's declaration, that at the day of judgment he will sentence the wicked to "go away into æonian punishment"; and that I also accept the representations which he and his apostles have made of the severities of that punishment. But I do not find it divinely revealed that the sufferings which sinners will be made to endure will be wholly and exclusively of the nature of *retributive inflictions.* If in any degree they shall be of that quality, every sinner will be dealt with according to his character and ill desert. No one will be made to suffer unjustly. No one will be punished beyond his desert. Every sufferer will see and feel that he deserves all he suffers.

But the *paramount object* of the punishment I am fain to believe will be the *reformation* of the sinner. This we know is the great object of all the severe and painful discipline to which God often subjects his creatures here in this world—not " for his own pleasure but for our profit, that we may be partakers of his holiness " ; and this I persuade myself will be the great object of the chastisements of the world to come. I can not help humbly lifting up my heart to the Infinite Father to sanction my hope and trust in the beneficent purpose of these Divine inflictions. And my thoughts frame themselves on this wise : O all-holy and all-merciful God ! thou hast not formed any of thy spiritual creatures for endless sin and wretchedness, but for goodness and blessedness. Thou hatest nothing that thou hast made, and dost forgive the sins of all those who are penitent. Thou desirest not the death of any sinner, but that he may turn to thee and live. This thou art perpetually declaring to us now—ever moving and drawing us by thy Holy Spirit working within us and by all the influences of thy good providence surrounding us here in this world. And why shouldst thou in the world to come abandon and cast off forever all thy creatures who may here in this world have withstood thy loving endeavors to turn them from sin ? Shall not thy love follow them there ? Wilt thou, after the short probation of this little life is over, utterly take thy Spirit

from them, and give them no further chance for
repentance and amendment? That be far from
thee, O Lord! I can not—I can not think of thee
as inexorably shutting thine ears to the cries for
mercy thy sinful children may raise to thee. Thou
mayst put them to sufferings in the world to
come. This thy Son hath disclosed in fearful
terms. But "God is love," and "our God is a
consuming fire." That fire, then, must needs be
a fire of love, however sharp the pain of it may
be—not a fire of hatred or of vengeance, but a
purifying and refining flame.

9. *Purgatory, but not the Romish one.*

I believe in *a* purgatory, but I reject the Romish doctrine concerning it, because it excludes from
the benefit of purgatorial discipline the souls of
such as die in what it calls "mortal sin"—terming
them "lost" souls, and consigning all such to endless torments in the place or state which it desig-
nates as hell; and, on the other hand, admits into
its purgatory only such as die in a state of grace,
obnoxious only to a "temporal (temporary) punishment," and whom it terms "pious souls."

Contrary to all this, I hold that a purgatorial
discipline is appointed for *all souls who need it*,
and in proportion to the degree and quality of
their need. The best of those who are not holy
enough to go immediately from death to the blessedness of heaven will not be exempted from any

needful severity of God's loving and merciful discipline, and the worst and wickedest of them will
not be excluded from its benefits.   All will be em-
braced within the scope of its beneficent Divine intention.   So I humbly presume to hope and trust.

Again, the doctrine of the Romish Church
goes upon the principle that after sinners have,
through repentance and faith, been freed from
the guilt and *endless* punishment incurred by sin,
there yet remains a "temporal punishment" *due
to Divine justice,* which must be endured either
in this world or in purgatory—unless it be remit-
ted, as in whole or in part it may be, on certain
conditions imposed by the Church.   In accordance
with this dogma the Romish Church represents
the sufferings appointed for souls in purgatory to
be wholly of the nature of penalties inflicted for
the satisfaction of a debt due to Divine *justice.*
I reject this representation, and I reject the dogma
it goes upon, as false and unrighteous in principle
and mischievous in its practical consequences—ly-
ing as it does at the basis of the whole scheme of
corrupt teaching and practice of the Romish Church
in the matter of indulgences, penances, satisfac-
tions, and all special conditions on which purgatorial pains and penalties may be mitigated, or
shortened, or altogether averted and evaded, in
virtue of an authority to that effect vested in the
priesthood of the Church—a most dangerous and
corrupting power, as the whole history of the Rom-

ish Church testifies. I reject this whole scheme.
I hold that the sufferings appointed to be endured
in the world beyond the grave are not of the nature of judicial penalties for the satisfaction of Divine justice, but are inflicted by God's fatherly
mercy as a reforming and purifying discipline.

10. Praying for the Dead.

I believe, moreover, that we may and should
pray for those who have passed away from this
life. To do so seems to me the spontaneous impulse of every kind and loving heart—an impulse
which will naturally prompt us first and most
strongly to intercede for those we have most ten-
derly loved and who have loved us here in this
life—to pray for such by name; an impulse that
will also prompt us to pray with like particularity
for those who have done us any wrong or had any
ill will toward us; and, finally, an impulse that
will prompt us to pray for the souls of *all* our
fellow creatures in the world beyond the grave.
I know that God knows what every one of them
has need of, and what methods of reforming discipline are suited precisely to each one's case. And
I think we may fervently implore his mercy upon
them in the humble, trustful hope that he will so
deal with them all as to purge them from sin and
establish them in that "holiness without which no
man shall see the Lord." Jesus has said, "If I be
lifted up upon the cross I will draw all men unto

me." And Holy Writ has declared that he shall see the travail of his soul and be satisfied. Can he ever be satisfied so long as there are souls for whom he died unreclaimed and unrestored? And can the love of the Infinite Father ever be satisfied so long as sin and the woe of it exist anywhere in his universe? Can he ever cease to work for its extinction?

If it be said that this goes to suggest and justify the idea of the final restoration to goodness and blessedness of not only all human spirits, but of all *superhuman* fallen and sinful spirits too, I can only say: Well, what then? Is not such a consummation one which every good and benevolent heart must be glad to believe in, if he may?

The "fallen angels," as they are called, are said in Scripture to be reserved in darkness and chains unto a day of judgment yet to come. But after that day how may it fare with them? They are, equally with human beings, the offspring of the love of the Almighty Father of all spirits, and higher, as is supposed, in original rank and endowments than we of the human race are. What if there be a dispensation of Divine mercy, hereafter to be disclosed, which shall include them all? Would not such a dispensation be in harmony with all that we know of the character and disposition of God? Can we, indeed, help thinking that God's love must needs prompt him to provide such a dispensation? At any

rate, I am sure of this much, that if any of God's
sinful children, anywhere throughout the universe, shall be finally lost, it will not be for lack
of anything he can do to reclaim them to goodness and to himself; and I can not but hope and
trust that he will employ the resources of his infinite power and wisdom so as in the end to bring
them all into a holy and blessed union with himself. But to return from this digression and go
on a little with the consideration of the sufferings
which may be ordained for sinful human beings
in the world beyond the grave.

11. Hell—Hades—Gehenna.

Hell—whether as the Hades or the Gehenna
of which our Lord has given us glimpses—I take
to be in its paramount intention a grand reforma-
tory institution with a discipline beneficently de-
signed to lead men through pain to penitence.
In what way it can and may work this end under
God's presiding providence and through the gracious influences of his good Spirit, he understands
better than I can, and I am persuaded that he
will order the discipline, in its quality and degree
and circumstances, according to the character and
peculiar needs of every soul that passes from this
life into the life beyond the grave. No doubt
there are many gradations of evil character in
hell, just as there are many gradations of holy
character in heaven. The poor rich man in the

parable was far from being wholly evil in character. With what eager unselfishness he begged that his five brethren might be warned of the consequences of living wholly luxurious, self-indulgent lives, so as not to come into the sad state of suffering he had sunk to! I am thankful for this trait which our Lord has introduced into the wonderful word picture he has painted.

There are many mansions in heaven, we are told, and I doubt not there are also many mansions in hell. Every dweller there will be put into the one he ought to be put into—the one that is best fitted for him; and will have to undergo there the sort and degree of purifying discipline which is necessary, fit, and most for his good—whether it be in the way of the natural consequences of sin (as we use the terms), or of specially appointed superaddition; whether it be from internal or external cause, or both. About all this it is idle to speculate. God, the sin-hating but sinner-loving God, will order all that.

But there is another point about which something may be said, namely, why it is that to us now living here in *this* world, under the dispensation of the gospel, our Lord has made such a disclosure of the sufferings to be endured by sinful men in the *world to come*. These representations are addressed not directly to our reason and conscience, but to our sensibilities; to the natural

dread with which we shrink from torturing pain.
But there is no quality of moral goodness in
shrinking from pain, none in merely being fright-
ened by the contemplation of the severities of
suffering which we ourselves may possibly have
to endure in the world to come; nor can the
dread of them have any morally salutary effect
upon us and upon our conduct here in this life,
except in so far as they serve to awaken and
quicken our consciences to a sense of the guilt
and ill desert of sin.

Our Lord's object in making these disclosures
doubtless was that they might have the effect of
quickening and deepening in us the conviction
that being wicked is in itself something far worse
than being punished for our wickedness; that the
evil character and disposition which necessarily
excludes the soul from union with its God is in
itself more dreadful than any outward punishment
we may imagine it to entail; so that in the end
we may become more desirous to gain deliverance
from the power of sin in this life than from its
punishment in the life beyond the grave.   In
such a disposition consists the essential and only
true salvation of the soul.   And such a disposition
will make us resign ourselves submissively to
whatever painful discipline Divine Wisdom and
Love may subject us to in this world or in the
world to come.

12. Through Pain to Penitence.

I doubt not the beneficent purpose, however imperfectly I may understand the connection between the means and the end. This I know, that God is not cruel. "He doth not willingly afflict or grieve the children of men." His inflictions are the chastisements of fatherly love—as in this world, so doubtless in the æonian world to come. It pains him to give us pain, even as it pains the good earthly father to punish his son for his son's own good. He no more takes delight in the pain he inflicts than the tender-hearted surgeon does when he cuts off his patient's limb to save his patient's life. Terribly have many, who have assumed to speak in God's name, misconstrued the purpose of the painful discipline ordained for sinful men in the world beyond the grave.

13. The Worm and the Fire.

The awful language in which our Lord (in Mark xi. 42-48) with six times reiterated warning bids us beware of the folly of incurring æonian sufferings in the life to come by sinful gratifications in this life, has been construed as declaring not only the *endlessness* of those sufferings (a point on which I have already said all that need be said), but that they are to be regarded as inflictions of *Divine wrath*, and the "worm that dieth not,"

and the "fire that is not quenched," as imaging
the infliction. But our Lord's language does not
necessarily contain any justification of the horrible
notion. On the contrary, it suggests and sanctions
the idea that these sufferings are a needful purifying discipline inflicted by the hand of the all-
merciful Father. Gehenna and its worm and
fire—to which Christ makes allusion—were a beneficent agency, consuming what would otherwise
have made the air of Jerusalem unfit for man to
breathe. Certain it is that such was the effect of
the wholesome worm and of the fire that was kept
burning day and night in the valley of Hinnom.

But what a picture of fiendish cruelties of torture inflicted by the *wrath* of God the fancy of Pollok has drawn in his " Course of Time " ! The un-
dying worm is a monster of the " serpent kind,"
with a thousand snaky heads and with as many
tails tipped with stings, and its mouths have each
a sting forked and long and venomous and sharp,
and in its infinite writhings malignantly grasping
human hearts quivering with torture, and making
vain efforts to avoid the transpiercing stings.

Equally horrible is the description of the lake
of burning fire into which sinful souls are remorse-
lessly plunged—miserable beings burning perpetually yet unconsumed, and forced to drink fre-
quent cups of burning gall, and filling their fiery
prison with howlings of woe and blasphemous
curses, to which the only response from above is

the inexorable refrain, " Ye knew your duty and
ye did it not." *

What an inspiration that which could prompt
such *poetic* (?) pictures of horror in honor of the
God of wrath !

In such a God I never can believe. I believe
in the God who *is* love, whose tender mercies are
supreme over all his works. The "wrath of the
Lamb " is a wrath of infinite Divine tenderness,
purifying us " as by fire "—a fire of love consuming our sinfulness to save our souls. " This universe," says a fervid writer, " is the theatre of
boundless and endless ministries of mercy, working through pain to blessed issues ; the love that
won the scepter on Calvary will wield it as a
power, waxing ever, waning never, through all
the ages ; the Father will never cease from yearn-
ing over the prodigals, and Christ will never cease
from seeking the lost while one knee remains
stubborn before the name of Jesus, and one heart
unmastered by his love." In this conviction " we
can face the vision of the terrible pain which sad-
dens the outlooks of life as disclosed in the Divine
Word." The burden, which would else be too
crushing for us, is lifted in a measure from our

---

* See, in the Appendix on " Orthodox Representations of
Future Punishment," the passages from Pollok's " Course of
Time," Book I., which I have referred to above. In that Appendix may be seen a *catena* of passages from prose writers not less
abominable in expression.

spirits, as we see around, above, beyond this dread experience the boundless and everlasting ministries of mercy drawing the sinner through the depths of anguish to the light, to the home, to the heart of God.*

14. Finale.

I leave off by repeating what I said at the outset of this letter. I humbly hope and trust that the endless existence of every human being will ultimately become one of endless goodness and blessedness. I can set no limits to the resources of the wisdom and power which infinite love must needs move the all-merciful Father to employ for the highest good of all his spiritual creatures. And throughout the ages of the never-ending future he has time enough to make trial of the inexhaustible riches of his grace. Must not evil in the end go down vanquished and destroyed by the all-conquering power of Divine love? In this hope I subscribe myself your ever-faithful friend,

C. S. HENRY.

* Baldwin Brown's "Doctrine of Annihilation in the Light of the Gospel of Love," p. 118.

APPENDICES.

APPENDIX I.

Modern Orthodox Representations of Future Punishment.

It is not worth while, for my purpose, to go into a particular recital of the opinions that prevailed in the early Church on the endless duration of future punishment. For five centuries it was regarded as an open question on which different opinions were held by Fathers of eminence and authority.

My particular purpose in this Appendix is to give some specimens of the views which have prevailed since the Reformation. For, strange as it may seem to many persons, the modern Protestant representations of hell and its torments have been more awful and revolting than those of the mediæval age. Hundreds of citations might be given in proof of it. I shall only cull out from the great mass such as I find in the books I happen to have in hand.

To begin with Calvin: "No description," says he, "can equal the severity of the Divine vengeance on the reprobate. . . . Harassed and agitated with a dreadful tempest, they shall feel themselves torn asunder by an angry God, and transfixed and penetrated by mortal stings, terrified by the thunderbolts of God, and broken by the weight of his hand : so that to sink into any gulfs and abysses would be more tolerable than to stand for a moment in these terrors. How great and severe, then, is the punishment to endure the never-ceasing effects of his wrath !" *

Take next some passages from Bishop Jeremy Taylor's discourse on " The Pains of Hell." " We are amazed," he says, " at the inhumanity of Phalaris, who roasted men in his brazen bull ; this was joy in respect of that fire of hell which penetrates the very entrails without consuming them. . . . Husbands shall see their wives, parents their children, tormented before their eyes. . . . The bodies of the damned shall be crowded together in hell like grapes in a wine-press which press one another till they burst. . . . Every distinct sense and organ shall be assailed with its own appropriate and most exquisite sufferings. Temporal fire is but a painted fire in respect of the penetrating and real fire in hell." †

Contemporary with Bishop Taylor, and not less famous, was Dr. Isaac Barrow, who describes

---

* Calvin's " Institutes," Book III., chapter xxv., § 12. See also Allen's translation, put out by the Presbyterian Board of Publication, vol. ii., p. 218.

† " Contemplation on the State of Man," chapters vi.–viii.

the future state of the wicked as that of being "detruded into utmost wretchedness; into a condition far more dark and dismal, more forlorn and disconsolate, than we can imagine; which not the sharpest pain of body, nor the bitterest anxiety of mind which any of us hath ever felt, can in any measure represent; wherein our bodies shall be afflicted continually by a sulphurous flame, not only scorching the skin, but piercing the inmost sinews." *

But nothing can surpass the frightful energy with which the celebrated Jonathan Edwards portrays the torments of the damned: "God holds sinners in his hands over the mouth of hell as so many spiders; and he is dreadfully provoked, and he not only hates them, but holds them in utmost contempt, and he will trample them under his feet with inexpressible fierceness; he will crush their blood out, and will make it fly so that he will sprinkle his garments and stain all his raiment." †   In another place he says: "The world will probably be converted into a great lake or liquid globe of fire—a vast ocean of fire, in which the wicked shall be overwhelmed, which will always be in tempest, in which they shall be tossed to and fro, having no rest day or night—vast waves or billows of fire continually rolling over their heads, of which they shall forever be full of

* Barrow's "Works," vol. v., p. 213.
† Edwards's "Works," vol. vii., p. 499.

a quick sense within and without; their heads, their eyes, their tongues, their hands, their feet, their loins, and their vitals shall forever be full of a glowing, melting fire, fierce enough to melt the very rocks and elements; and also they shall eternally be full of the most quick and lively sense to feel the torments; not for one minute, nor for one day, nor for one age, nor for two ages, nor for a hundred ages, nor for ten thousands of millions of ages one after another, but forever and ever, without any end at all, and never, never be delivered." *

What wonder is it that such terrific utterances had the effect they are said to have had upon those who heard them—believing, as they did, the truth of every word they heard? "Whole congregations," as Edwards's biographers relate, "shuddered and simultaneously rose to their feet, smiting their breasts, weeping and groaning." † And what wonder is it that theologians and preachers who could paint a God so fiendish as to take delight in the torments of the wicked in hell, should represent the blessed dwellers in heaven as finding an equally fiendish delight in the horrible spectacle? This shocking notion was first put out— so far as I know—in the thirteenth century, by St. Thomas Aquinas, who said, "In order that the saints may enjoy their beatitude more richly,

* Edwards's "Works," vol. viii., p. 166.
† Alger's "Doctrine of a Future Life," p. 517.

a perfect sight of the punishment of the damned is granted to them." The Puritans of a later period seemed to revel in the idea that " the joys of the blessed were to be deepened and sharpened by constant contrast with the sufferings of the damned." Jonathan Edwards thus expresses the same thought : " The sight of hell torments will exalt the happiness of the saints forever. It will not only make them more sensible of the greatness and freeness of the grace of God in their own happiness, but it will really make their happiness the greater, as it will make them more sensible of their own happiness; it will give them a more lively relish for it ; it will make them prize it more. A sense of the opposite misery in any case greatly increases the relish of any joy or pleasure." *

But the celebrated New England divine, Dr. Samuel Hopkins, contemporary with Edwards and his biographer, has given perhaps the most intense expression to the frightful idea. Of the wicked he says: " The smoke of their torment shall ascend up in the sight of the blessed forever and ever, and serve as a most clear glass always before their eyes to give them a bright and most affecting view. This display of the Divine character will be *most entertaining* [!] to all who love God, and will give them the highest and most ineffable pleasure. Should the fire of this eternal

---

* Edwards's " Works," vol. iii., p. 276.

punishment cease, it would in a great measure obscure the light of heaven, and put an end to a great part of the happiness and glory of the blessed." *

Coming now into our own century, let us see what of like sort we find. The eminent American divine and preacher, Dr. Gardiner Spring, not long since gone from the earth, said: "The souls of all who have died in their sins are in hell, and there their bodies will be after the resurrection. . . . When the omnipotent and angry God, who has access to all the avenues of distress in the corporeal frame, and all the inlets to agony in the intellectual constitution, undertakes to punish, he will convince the universe that he does not gird himself for the work of retribution in vain. . . . It will be *a glorious deed* when he who hung on Calvary shall cast those who have trodden his blood under their feet into the furnace of fire where there shall be weeping and wailing and gnashing of teeth." †

The celebrated John Henry Newman, in his sermon on the "Neglect of Divine Calls and Warnings," says of one of the damned: "His soul is in hell, O ye children of men! While thus ye speak, his soul is in the beginning of those torments in which his body will soon have part,

* Park's "Memoir of Hopkins," pp. 201, 202. Hopkins died in 1802, at the age of eighty-two.
† "The Glory of Christ," vol. ii., p. 258.

and which will never die." * And Mr. Spurgeon, another famous living writer and preacher, in his graphic and fearful sermon on "The Resurrection of the Dead," says : "When thou diest thy soul will be tormented alone ; that will be a hell for it : but at the day of judgment thy body will join thy soul, and then thou wilt have twin hells, thy soul sweating drops of blood and thy body suffused with agony. In fire, exactly like that which we have on earth, thy body will lie, asbestus-like, forever unconsumed, all thy veins roads for the feet of Pain to travel on, every nerve a string on which the devil shall forever play his diabolical tune of 'Hell's Unutterable Lament.'" †

The woes of hell had in the mediæval age their poet in Dante. In the present age they have found one in Robert Pollok. As *poets* I do not compare them, for who would think of naming them together? But the pictures in the "Inferno" are less coarsely and revoltingly horrible than in Pollok's "Course of Time." Take his portrait of the "*worm that never dies*" :

"... But how shall I describe
What naught resembles else my eye hath seen ?
Of worm or serpent kind it something looked,
But monstrous, with a thousand snaky heads,
Eyed each with double orbs of glaring wrath ;
And with as many tails, that twisted out

* *Vide* Alger, "Doctrine of a Future Life," p. 520.
† Ibid., p. 518.

In horrid revolution, tipped with stings;
And all its mouths, that wide and darkly gaped,
And breathed most poisonous breath, had each a sting
Forked, and long, and venomous, and sharp;
And in its writhings infinite it grasped
Malignantly what seemed a heart swollen, black,
And quivering with torture most intense;
And still the heart, with anguish throbbing high,
Made effort to escape, but could not; for
Howe'er it turned, and oft it vainly turned,
These complicated foldings held it fast.
And still the monstrous beast with sting of head
Or tail transpierced it bleeding evermore.
What this could image much I searched to know,
And while I stood and gazed and wondered long,
A voice from whence I know not, for no one
I saw, distinctly whispered in my ear
These words—' *This is the worm that never dies!* '"

To the foregoing citations I will only further add something respecting the fate of infants and of the heathen.

Calvin assumes the truth of the doctrine of infant damnation in that celebrated, often-quoted passage in his " Institutes," where he says, " That the fall of Adam should involve so many nations with their *infant children* in eternal death : .... is, I confess, an awful decree," * which yet he justifies as the result of that Divine predestination " whereby God has determined in himself what he would have to become of every individual of

* " Institutes," Book III., chapter xxiv., § 12.—Allen's translation, vol. ii., p. 170.

mankind. For they are not all created with a
similar destiny; but eternal life is forcordained
for some, and eternal damnation for others "; and
that "to those whom he devotes to condemnation
the gate of life is closed by a just and irreprehen-
sible but incomprehensible judgment." *

The Lutheran doctrine, as expressed in the
" Augsburg Confession," teaches that, " after the
fall of Adam, all men who are naturally born are
born in sin ; that is, born with evil desires, etc. ;
and this disease or original vitiosity is truly sin,
damnable and entailing the wrath of God and
eternal death on all who are not regenerated by
baptism by the Holy Spirit." † Mosheim, the
eminent Lutheran divine of the last century, says :
" This depravity of our nature, although it is in-
voluntary in us and derived from our first parents,
is nevertheless imputed to us as sin in the chan-
cery of heaven. *Wherefore, if no other sin were
added, we should be exposed to Divine punishment,
on account of this depravity itself.*" ‡

In somewhat softened phrase, evangelical Lu-
therans of a later day say : " Even the souls of
those who on account of their innate depravity die
in their infancy, although they are themselves in-
nocent, still participate in some degree in the punishment inflicted on Adam, inasmuch as they are

---

* Allen's translation, vol. ii., pp. 145, 149.
† " Sylloge Confessionum," Oxon., 1827, p. 166.
‡ Mosheim, " Elements of Dogmatic Theology," vol. i., p. 540.

justly regarded to be unworthy to be fellow members of the society of angels and the just made
perfect in the kingdom of heaven, and partakers
of the blessedness which they enjoy." *

As to the fate of the heathen, take the decla-
rations of the American Board of Commissioners
for Foreign Missions—as I find them in "Alger's
"Doctrine of a Future Life." I am not able to lay
my hand on the official documents, but there is
no reason whatever to suppose the quotations have
not been correctly made.

"To send the gospel to the heathen," say these
commissioners, "is a work of great exigency.
Within the last thirty years a whole generation of
five hundred millions have gone down to eternal
death." Again, the same Board say in their tract
entitled "The Grand Motive to Missionary Effort": "The heathen are involved in the ruins of
the apostasy, and are expressly doomed to perdition. Six hundred millions of deathless souls on
the brink of hell! What a spectacle!" An American missionary to China said, in a public address
after his return : "Fifty thousand a day go down
to the fire that is not quenched. Six hundred
millions more are going the same road. Should
you not think at least once a day of the fifty thousand who that day sink to the doom of the lost?" †

---

* Storr and Flatt, "Biblical Theology," Schmucker's edition,
Andover, 1826, vol. ii., p. 59.

† Alger, "Doctrine of a Future Life," p. 544.

What a frightful contemplation is offered to our minds if it be true (as is here alleged) that ignorance of Christ and consequent want of an explicit faith in him entail the endless perdition of the soul! In the upshot it comes to this: that not only fifty thousand go daily down to an endless hell, but the great bulk of mankind for the four thousand years before Christ came and for the two thousand years since he came have gone there. As I roughly compute it, a hundred and fifty thousand millions of human beings have come into existence here on the earth and passed away by death; and of these the vast majority are now in hell, and doomed to abide there forever, for not believing in a Saviour they never heard of! I thank God neither our mother Church of England nor her American daughter requires me to hold or to preach any such doctrine, although I have heard it preached by ministers of both.

The sketch I have given of the "Orthodox" notions on future punishment from the commencement of the Reformation to the present time will, I think, justify the statement that the modern Protestant doctrine is far more hideous and revolting than anything taught in Christendom during the ancient or the mediæval period.

APPENDIX II.

Mediæval Opinion.[*]

THROUGHOUT the middle ages the world after death continued to reveal more fully its awful secrets. Hell, purgatory, and heaven, became more distinct—if it may be so said, more visible. Their site, their topography, their torments, their trials, their enjoyments, became more conceivable, almost more palpable to sense; till Dante summed up the whole of this traditional lore, or at least, with a poet's intuitive sagacity, seized on all which was most imposing, effective, real, and condensed it in his three coördinate poems. That hell had a local existence, that immaterial spirits suffered bodily and material torments, none, or scarcely one hardy speculative mind, presumed to doubt. Hell admitted, according to legend, more than one visitant from this upper world who returned to relate his fearful journey to wondering man: St. Fiercy, St. Vettin, a layman Bernilo. But all these early descents interest us only as they may be supposed or appear to have been faint types of

[*] Extract from Milman's "Latin Christianity," pp. 221-227.

the great Italian poet. Dante is the one authorized topographer of the mediæval hell. IIis origi-
nality is no more called in question by these mere
signs and manifestations of the popular belief than
by the existence and reality of those objects or
scenes in external nature which he describes with
such unrivaled truth. In Dante meet unrecon-
ciled (who thought or cared for their reconcilia-
tion ?) those strange contradictions—immaterial
souls subject to material torments; spirits which
had put off the mortal body cognizable by the corporeal sense. The mediæval hell had gathered
from all ages, all lands, all races, its imagery, its
denizens, its site, its access, its commingling hor-
rors: from the old Jewish traditions, perhaps from
regions beyond the sphere of the Old Testament;
from the pagan poets with their black rivers, their
Cerberus, their boatman, his crazy vessel; perhaps
from Teutonic IIela through some of the earlier
visions. Then came the great poet, and reduced
all this wild chaos to a kind of order, molded it
up with the cosmical notions of the times, and
made it, as it were, one with the prevalent mun-
dane system. Above all, he brought it to the very
borders of our world; he made the life beyond
the grave one with our present life; he mingled
in close and intimate relation the present and the
future. IIell, purgatory, heaven, were but an immediate expansion and extension of the present
world. And this is among the wonderful causes

of Dante's power, the realizing the unreal by the admixture of the real—even as in his imagery the actual, homely, every-day language or similitude mingles with and heightens the fantastic, the vague, the transmundane. What effect had hell produced, if peopled by ancient, almost immemorial objects of human detestation, Nimrod or Iscariot, or Julian or Mohammed? It was when popes all but living, kings but now on their thrones, Guelphs who had hardly ceased to walk the streets of Florence, Ghibellines almost yet in exile, revealed their awful doom—this it was which, as it expressed the passions and the fears of mankind of an instant, immediate, actual, bodily, comprehensive place of torment : so wherever it was read, it deepened that notion and made it more distinct and natural. This was the hell conterminous to the earth, but separate, as it were, by a gulf passed by almost instantaneous transition, of which the priesthood held the keys. These keys the audacious poet had wrenched from their hands, and dared to turn on many of themselves, speaking even against popes the sentence of condemnation. Of that which hell, purgatory, heaven, were in the popular opinion during the middle ages, Dante was but the full, deep, concentrated expression ; what he embodied in verse all men believed, feared, hoped.

Purgatory had now its intermediate place between heaven and hell as unquestioned, as undisturbed by doubt; its existence was as much an article of uncontested popular belief as heaven or hell. It were as unjust and unphilosophical to attribute all the legendary lore which realized purgatory to the sordid invention of the churchman or the monk, as it would be unhistorical to deny the use which was made of this superstition to extract tribute from the fears or the fondness of mankind. But the abuse grew out of the belief; the belief was not slowly, subtly instilled into the mind for the sake of the abuse. Purgatory, possible with St. Augustine, probable with Gregory the Great, grew up, I am persuaded (its growth is singularly indistinct and untraceable), out of the mercy and modesty of the priesthood. To the eternity of hell torments there is and ever must be—notwithstanding the peremptory decrees of dogmatic theology and the reverential dread in so many religious minds of tampering with what seems the language of the New Testament—a tacit repugnance. But when the doom of every man rested on the lips of the priest, on his absolution or refusal of absolution, that priest might well tremble with some natural awe—awe not confessed to himself—at dismissing the soul to an irrevocable, unrepealable, unchangeable destiny. He would not be averse to pronounce a more mitigated, a revisable sentence. The keys of heaven and of hell were a fearful trust, a terrible responsibility; the key of purgatory might be used with far less presumption, with less trembling confidence. Then came naturally, as might seem, the strengthening and exaltation of the efficacy of prayer, of the efficacy of the sacrifice of the altar, and the efficacy of the intercession of the saints: and these all within the province, within the power of the sacerdotal order. Their authority, their influence, their intervention, closed not with the grave. The departed soul was still to a certain degree dependent upon the priest. They had yet a mission, it might be of mercy; they had still some power of saving the soul after it had departed from the body. Their faithful love, their inexhaustible interest, might yet rescue the sinner; for he had not reached those gates over which alone was written, " There is no hope "—the gates of hell. That which was a mercy, a consolation, became a trade, an inexhaustible source of wealth. Praying souls out of purgatory, by masses said on their behalf, became an ordinary office, an office which deserved, which could demand, which did demand, the most prodigal remuneration. It was later that the indulgence, originally the remission of so much penance, of so many days, weeks, months, years; or of that which was the commutation for penance, so much almsgiving or munificence to churches or to churchmen, in sound at least extended (and mankind, the high and low vulgar of mankind, are governed by sound) its significance; it was literally understood, as the remission of so many years, sometimes centuries, of purgatory.

If there were living men to whom it had been vouchsafed to visit and return and reveal the secrets of remote and terrible hell, there were those too who were admitted in vision or in actual life to more accessible purgatory, and brought back intelligence of its real local existence, and of the state of souls within its penitential circles. There is a legend of St. Paul himself; of the French monk St. Farcy; of Drithelm, related by Bede; of the Emperor Charles the Fat, by William of Malmesbury. Matthew Paris relates two or three journeys of the monk of Evesham, of Thurkill, an Essex peasant, very wild and fantastic. The purgatory of St. Patrick, the purgatory of Owen Miles, the vision of Alberic of Monte Casino, were among the most popular and wide-spread legends of the ages preceding Dante; and as in hell, so in purgatory, Dante sums up in his noble verses the whole theory, the whole popular belief, as to this intermediate sphere.

APPENDIX III.

Recent Roman Catholic Representations.

OXENHAM's " Catholic Eschatology, an Essay on the Doctrine of Future Retribution " (London, 1876), is devoted to a vindication of the dogma of the endless punishment of the lost. I give here some extracts from it :

" . . . . The causes which have mainly contributed to foster, even in religious and reverential minds, a repugnance to the dogma of eternal punishment, I believe may, broadly speaking, be reduced to two.

" In the first place, all sorts of popular opinions or fancies—pure *idola fori*, as they may be termed, and which at best are but accidental accessories of the doctrine—have got mixed up with it in men's minds till they have almost lost sight of its essential meaning. Such are various notions about the place and the exact nature of future punishment, of physical torture, material fire, and the like, which may or may not be true,

but are matters of speculation only, on which in
all ages different opinions have been maintained
by theologians of unimpeached orthodoxy. . . .
One point it may be well to notice at once, because to many minds it has seemed to invest the
whole doctrine with peculiar horror. There is
something shocking to our natural instincts in the
damnation of unbaptized infants, understood in a
coarse and popular sense. . . . But no such mon-
strosity is involved in the Catholic doctrine. . . .
But the most conspicuous example of this care-
less or insidious confusion between the essence of
the dogma and its purely separable accidents, and
which has probably done more than all other mis-
conceptions put together to prejudice men's minds
against it, remains to be noticed. . . . I am not
acquainted with a single Universalist writer who
does not argue as though the doctrine he is assail-
ing" (the doctrine of eternal punishment) "involved the damnation of the *great majority* of
mankind . . . . the damnation not only of unbaptized infants, . . . but of the entire heathen
world. . . . The damnation of the entire heathen world, both before and since incarnation, became a necessary corollary of the fundamental
tenets of the Reformers, and was openly proclaimed as such. And the recoil from a conclusion shocking to the mind, and drawn from
premises alike unphilosophical and heterodox,
contributed not a little to the attack on a dog-

ma" (eternal punishment) "which is in no wise responsible for that conclusion.

".... I am brought to the second and most far-reaching and effective of the two causes just now referred to as having mainly influenced religious minds in their revolt against the revealed doctrine of eternal punishment. That cause lies in the neglect or denial among Protestants of another great Christian truth, attested by heathen philosophy and tradition, no less than by the teaching of the Church, and of which it may be said with terrible emphasis *neglectum sui ulcisitur*. I mean the doctrine of purgatory and prayer for the departed. It is certainly a strange Nemesis on those who for upward of three centuries have been inveighing against this doctrine as a pagan superstition, to find themselves constrained suddenly to turn round upon us with the charge that we are teaching 'horrible' and 'infamous' doctrines, and are no better than 'priests of Moloch' if we decline to accept at their bidding a universal purgatory for everybody. . . . In spite, however, of this overwhelming weight of external authority and of the elementary instincts of natural religion, the Reformers . . . . made short work of purgatory and prayer for the dead. And if the Church of England is not committed to any express denial of the doctrine, every trace of it was studiously expunged from the revised Prayer-Book of 1552, and under this authorized desuetude it dropped—gradually, perhaps, but inevitably—out of the religious faith and practice of the multitude. There must always have been many who, like Dr. Johnson, interceded privately for their lost ones, while many more who dared not rebel against the tyranny of a false tradition groaned in secret under the perverse refinement of superstitious cruelty which, in the hour of darkness and desolation, when all earthly lights are darkened and the stricken heart instinctively turns to God, sternly forbade them to name before him mother, or wife, or child, or beloved friend, whose name till then had never been absent from their daily prayers. It is customary with Anglicans to talk of 'our beautiful burial service,' and beautiful no doubt it is, so far as language goes; naturally enough, for nearly every word of it, not contained in the text of Scripture, is taken from Catholic sources. Its fault is not of commission but of omission, but it is a radical one. It has often been my lot to hear that service read over the graves of those very dear to me, and at such times I have never been able to escape a bitter sense of the unreality of a ritual, however musical in expression, which consigns their bodies to the earth without one syllable of intercession for their parted souls.* A service

---

* With such pedantic and rigid minuteness is this principle carried out, that while solemn commendation of the body to the earth is still retained, the accompanying commendation of the

for the dead which omits to pray for them is indeed, to use the hackneyed simile, like ‘Hamlet’ with the Prince of Denmark left out! And this cold neglect of intercession for the departed has induced a thoroughly false habit of mind regarding their present condition and our relation to them. . . .

“It is in no spirit of captiousness or theological partisanship that I refer to the matter here, nor is it even chiefly in order to emphasize the grave neglect of one of the most obvious and urgent obligations of Christian charity, which has thus been introduced and perpetuated for centuries. But I wished to call attention to the indirect results of this denial of purgatory and consequent disuse of prayer for the departed. . . . Let it be granted—as is implied in the Tridentine decree on the subject—that errors or abuses had crept into the current teaching about purgatory, as there were also erroneous opinions afloat about the efficacy of good works. That was a good reason for explaining, not for rejecting, the doctrines which had been misunderstood. Anglicans at least might be expected to remember the principle which Hooker uses with so much effect against his Puritan assailants, that ‘the abuse of a thing taketh not away the lawful use thereof.’ But just as Luther in his misguided zeal for the interests

soul to “God the Father Almighty,” found in Edward VI.’s First Book, was struck out by the Puritan revisers of 1552.

of morality invented a new theory of justification, which is proved by reason and experience to be profoundly immoral, so did the rejection of purgatory on the part of the Reformers determine, by an inevitable recoil, the revolt of their children against that dogma of eternal punishment to which they hoped thereby to give additional prominence.

"We can not wonder that it should be so. If the disembodied spirit passes straight from the death-bed to its eternal home, the difficulties of the received belief become wellnigh insuperable. How few comparatively are there who, even to our clouded and partial apprehension, appear fit at the moment of departure for the presence into which nothing that is defiled can enter! And to imagine, as Möhler expresses it, some mechanical effect in the mere 'act of deliverance from the body,' or 'magical change' immediately following it, is an hypothesis as arbitrary and unphilosophical as it is wholly destitute of Scriptural support. . . .

". . . . The difficulty is met by the Catholic doctrine of purgatory. For the sufferings of that intermediate state, as Möhler is careful to insist, are no mere mechanical infliction, nor can the sufferer be regarded as other than a voluntary agent in the working out of his own final purification. . . . The will coöperates actively in the divine process whereby the remains of evil habits and inclinations are gradually purged away, till the perfect image of Christ is reproduced in the soul, and it is made fit for the beatific vision and the inheritance of the saints in light. . . . Sometimes the work is complete in this life, but oftener it is not. Years or centuries of corrective discipline may be required for some. . . .

"But since Christ was crucified no soul of man, not dying in infancy, was ever sanctified without suffering, whether its fire-baptism be endured in this life or in the world beyond the grave.

". . . . Purgatory serves to illustrate the awful purity and tender compassion of our God. It witnesses to that perfect holiness without which none may see his face, and to the long-suffering charity which would still at the eleventh hour 'devise a way to bring his banished home.' We may not dare to penetrate the secrets of his providence, but we may thankfully gaze with hope as well as awe on what Faber has somewhere beautifully called that 'eighth great sacrament of fire,' and trust it will avail for the final purification of countless millions who have partially misused or neglected or been inculpably deprived of the seven sacraments of earth. When we contemplate, for instance, the multitudes of this huge metropolis, and consider how large is the proportion of them who . . . . are born into an atmosphere charged with impurity and blasphemy, and often, after a few short years of coarse and godless frivolity or unsolaced suffering, sink into an early and what

looks like a hopeless grave, the spectacle would
indeed be a heart-rending one if we had not reason to believe that for many of these also, who in
the unerring judgment of the great Discerner of
hearts have not sinned fatally against the light,
there may remain that second baptism of fire to
anneal them for the presence they had never been
taught to recognize on earth. In vast numbers of
those neglected children, the street Arabs of our
overgrown cities, are latent, we can not doubt, the
same admirable moral capabilities which were so
nobly exemplified the other day by the boys on
the Goliath, and those who know most of them
assure us that it is so; but too often, from adverse
circumstances and lack of opportunity, their better
qualities remain undeveloped to the last in this
world. And thus what, as regards ourselves, is a
prospect full of the deepest awe, and a keen in-
centive to work out our salvation while it is yet
day, enables us to judge hopefully of the future
possibilities of others whose temptations may be
stronger and their opportunities far less than ours,
but of whom it were no true charity to doubt that
they are not at present such as God would have
them.

"Take again the case of what are called death-
bed conversions. I am far from denying that such
things are possible, and may not be uncommon,
though there is not perhaps much evidence to
show it. The operations of grace can not be lim-

4

ited by measurements of earthly time, and in that
last hour of his extremest need the prodigal may
heed the call so long neglected, return to his
Father's arms, and die forgiven. But the habits
and associations of a lifetime are not so easily un-
learned, and the work of sanctification has still
to be accomplished. The soul has all the scars of
its old sins and corrupt tastes and dispositions still
upon it; it is 'not pure nor strong enough for
bliss,' and must be cleansed and braced and per-
fected in the fires of God's righteous correction before it can bear the unclouded sunshine of his love.

" On whichever side it is looked at, the doctrine of purgatory is a most helpful, most consol-
ing, most practical, most fruitful, most suggestive,
most indispensable truth. We can hardly make
too much of it so long as we do not confound the
salutary discipline of that intermediate trial-place
with the worm that dieth not and the fire that is
not quenched. So directly did the Reformers contradict the instincts of natural religion as well as
the testimony of revelation in their denial of this
truth, that many who had been brought up in their
tenets rebelled against it. . . .

". . . . But without the recognized and regu-
lar practice of prayer for the departed, which is
its correlative, it can not be expected to take root
in the popular belief. Its standing witness is
found in the sacrifice of the mass."—(" Catholic Eschatology," etc., pp. 14–40.)

APPENDIX IV.

Alexander Ewing, Bishop of Argyll and the Isles.

Mr. Ross has given us a memoir of that most loving and lovable man, from which I extract a few sentences:

"It is good, surely," says Mr. Ross, "to reproduce so far as may be the history of a radiant, sympathizing human soul who, much loved and greatly honored, knew how to infuse a fresh charm into the life not only of his fireside circle, but into that of the casual acquaintance on board a steamer, and who, endowed with a truly Highland chivalry, stood ever ready to come to the front in the battle-field of human progress. But over and above these considerations Dr. Ewing had a special message to deliver to his fellow men on the most important of all subjects—on the character of God, the mission of Christ, the discipline of life, and life's ultimate issues. A theologian, indeed, was Alexander Ewing—a theologian who had become a little child, and listened reverently and humbly at the feet of Christ as he spoke to his heart, to all that was best in him of a Father in

heaven who is ' perfect '—that was the word which
made all things new for him. He had read, no
doubt, of the measureless significance of this attribute in the writings of Thomas Erskine, but it
was the great assertion of the redemption of mankind contained in the English Prayer-Book which
first broke up within him, beneath the crust of
traditional dogma, the fountain of theological speculation. . . .

".... ' The God of the New Testament,' says
Niebuhr, in words which Neander has made known
to all men, ' is " heart to heart." ' That truth is
the key-note of all Bishop Ewing's teaching. He
has no poor apologies to offer for his creed. He
has no dismal compromises to effect between at-
tributes, so called, of the divine nature. To him
God is light—all light; his justice is light, his
mercy is light . . . . its light is its own evidence,
streaming into the heart and conscience that are
kindred with it, and rejoice in it when once be-
held, as the natural eye rejoiceth in the light of
the sun. Incipient loyalty to Christ forbade him
to doubt the truth of the words, ' He that follow-
eth me shall not walk in darkness, but shall see
the light of life.' . He proved the words. He gave
himself to Christ as the Lord of meekness, of sin-
gleness of vision, of childlike, all-trustful, all-sub-
missive uplooking. He was alone with the Alone,
but with Christ as his guide ; and the Father who
seeth in secret was ' himself ' his reward. He

found the secret of his creation—his own and that of all men. He learned to say ' *Our* Father,' and the inference which Christ teaches us to draw came upon his surprised and at first all but incredulous spirit with life-long power: ' If ye, then, being evil, know how to give good gifts to your children, how much more shall your heavenly Father give all good things to them that ask him?'—*how much more?* Bishop Ewing felt himself borne up by these words into a regenerating newness of hope which no words could ever do more than faintly shadow. To the question, ' How much more?' his one response was, 'Infinitely more,' and hence he writes: 'God, seen as our Father, makes all things sweet, all paths straight, reconciles all things. This Fatherhood, once truly accepted, solves all perplexities, and makes the difficulties of life clear and plain. He is our Father, and, whatever is meant by that name, that is he and always so. Life, death, make no alteration in this relationship. In life, after death, he is equally the same, and Father. Beyond the shores of death we do not go into a strange country; it is still our Father's house, where the Father is dealing with his children as they require. No time, no space, can destroy his eternal, uniform, and paternal relation."

THE END.

www.ingramcontent.com/pod-product-compliance
Lightning Source LLC
Chambersburg PA
CBHW030020030726
47499CB00008B/3060